Sylvie McSlipper

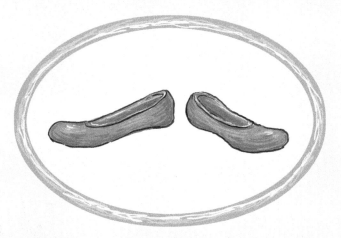

By Nancy Alfaro

Illustrated by Helena Chatlain

Dedicated to my Bunnie,
Skye Lilly Torres.
−NA

To LLL, with thanks.
−HSC

Sylvie McSlipper had hundreds of shoes
to all those who knew her
this wasn't new news.

Deep in her closet her shoes towered high.
They looked like they'd burst
through the roof to the sky!

Yes, Sylvie had so many shoes, but why?

She had **PINK** shoes and **BLUE** shoes and

SNOW shoes
and TOE shoes

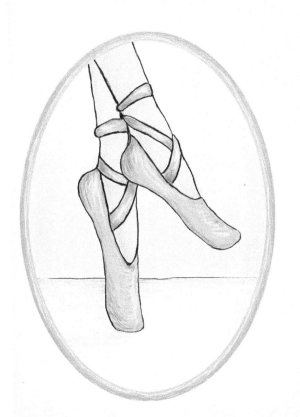

She even had some
INVISIBLE
no shoes!

and **RED** shoes

and **WHITE** shoes

and taxi-cab

YELLOW

She even had one pair the color of JELL-O!

The shoes in her closet were piled up high.
Yes, Sylvie had so many shoes.
But why?

Her dad,
Sam McSlipper,
made everyone's
shoes!

Even Chippy McChipper's —
he's got some in BLUE.

Yes Sam McSlipper, was the SHOE KING.
He made everyone's shoes for

fall

winter

spring!

When it came to the summertime,
he took a break
and thought of new styles
that one day he'd make.

Yes, Mr. McSlipper was the
SHOE KING.
He made everyone's shoes for
fall, winter, and spring.

Once the school year began, almost everyday
Sylvie went to dad's workbench,
where she loved to play.

"Where's
funny Ms. Carrie?"
she'd run in and say.

"Oh dear little Sylvie, she is downstairs.
She'll give you more shoes,
maybe twenty-five pairs!"

"But Sylvie darling, I'm starting to think:
Maybe kids with no shoes
is of whom you should think."

"What d'you mean daddy,
why can't I have them?"

"We'll talk of it later.
Go downstairs,
go grab them."

Sylvie McSlipper
ran fast down the stairs.
She ran down to look
at her twenty-five pairs.

Maybe she'd find GLITTER sneakers to wear!

Funny Ms. Carrie put shoes in a bag.
The bag was so big
that it had to be dragged.

They emptied it onto her dad's office floor.
That's when he said,
"Sylvie, please shut the door."

"Ok my daddy, but what did I do?"

"It's not what you did dear,
these shoes just can't stay.
It's time that you pick some,
and give most away."

"There are children
who walk with
no shoes on their feet,"
said funny Ms. Carrie
not missing a beat.

"I should have told you this way before,"
said funny Ms. Carrie as she opened the door.

"I'm glad that you told me
just when you did,
for now I can give shoes
to many a kid!"

And Sylvie McSlipper went right to that pile
and stared at her shoes for a little while.

"I have enough shoes at home to spare,
I'll give ALL these away, it's only fair."

She pictured her closet at home filled with shoe
and knew there were many that she'd never use.

"When I get home later
I'll pick and I'll choose,
I'll help loads of kids get brand new shoes."

Daddy hugged her, and hugged her,
and said in her ear,
"I'm PROUD of you Sylvie,
you'll bring so much cheer."

And home they both ran
   to take down the shoe tower.

The tower of BLUE shoes

and PINK shoes

and WHITE

and shoes that inside of the heel had a LIGHT.

The **BOAT** shoes

and **SKI BOOTS**

and **SILVERY** sandals.

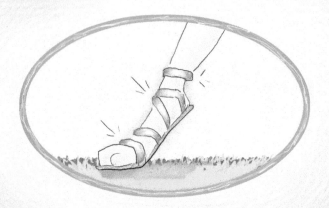

Sylvie even had shoes like a teapot with **HANDLES!**

And her tower
of shoes got

lower

and lower

until there were only two pair,
one with flowers.

"I am so happy to help other kids,
I'm Sylvie McSlipper, and look what I did!"

THE END

Do you have shoes
that you don't often use?
Just like Sylvie YOU can
help other kids, too!

Learn more at
www.soles4souls.org

Nancy Alfaro

Author

Nancy Alfaro is the author of
numerous magazine features
and reviews. Alfaro lives, works
and writes, in New York City.
Sylvie McSlipper is her first
children's book.

@iamsylviemcslipper

Helena Chatlain

Illustrator

Helena is a lover of painting
and illustrating. She calls
Alaska home, where she lives
with her twins and their piles
of shoes! This is her first book.
You can see some of her
other art on Instagram:
@hscpaint

CPSIA information can be obtained
at www.ICGtesting.com
Printed in the USA
BVHW022034140921
616277BV00007B/5

9 781736 151517